Old MacDonald had a farm, ee-i-ee-i-o!

And on that farm he had a dog.

Ee-i-ee-i-o!

Old MacDonald had a farm, ee-i-ee-i-o!
And on that farm he had a pig.

Ee-i-ee-i-o!

Woof! Woof!
here an oink!
there an oink!
Oink!
Piggy Potty
Everywhere an oink oink!

Old MacDonald had a farm, ee-i-ee-i-o!
And on that farm he had a cow.

Ee-i-ee-i-o!

Old MacDonald had a farm, ee-i-ee-i-o!
And on that farm he had a sheep.

Ee-i-ee-i-o!

Old MacDonald had a farm, ee-i-ee-i-o!
And on that farm he had a cat.

Ee-i-ee-i-o!

Old MacDonald had a farm, ee-i-ee-i-o!
And on that farm he had a horse.

Ee-i-ee-i-o!

Old MacDonald had a farm, ee-i-ee-i-o!
And on that farm he had a turkey.

Ee-i-ee-i-o!

Old MacDonald had a farm, ee-i-ee-i-o!
And on that farm he had an . . .

I bet you didn't know!

Old MacDonald had a farm . . .

EEE-I-EEE-I-OOO!

Other books in the series:

I KNOW AN OLD LADY WHO SWALLOWED A FLY
NOAH BUILT AN ARK ONE DAY

First published in Great Britain 1991
by Methuen Children's Books Ltd
Published 1992 by Little Mammoth.
Reprinted 1992, 1994.
Reissued 1999 by Mammoth
an imprint of Egmont Children's Books Ltd.
239 Kensington High Street, London, W8 6SL
10 9 8 7 6 5 4 3 2 1

A CIP catalogue record for this title is available from the British Library

ISBN 0 7497 0603 1

Printed in Malaysia